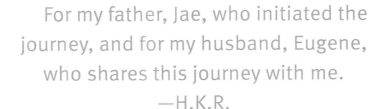

For my father, Jae, who initiated the
journey, and for my husband, Eugene,
who shares this journey with me.
—H.K.R.

To Lily, Max and Colin. I love you.
To Katrina, I love you.
Thank you for being everything.
—P.C.

Text copyright © 2022 by Helena Ku Rhee
Jacket art and interior illustrations copyright © 2022 by Pascal Campion

All rights reserved. Published in the United States by Random House Studio,
an imprint of Random House Children's Books,
a division of Penguin Random House LLC, New York.

Random House Studio with colophon is a trademark of Penguin Random House LLC.

Visit us on the Web!
rhcbooks.com

Educators and librarians, for a variety of teaching tools, visit us at RHTeachersLibrarians.com

Library of Congress Cataloging-in-Publication Data is available upon request.
ISBN 978-0-593-37549-5 (trade) — ISBN 978-0-593-37550-1 (lib. bdg.) — ISBN 978-0-593-37551-8 (ebook)

The text of this book is set in 15-point Meta Pro Book.
Interior design by Sarah Hokanson

MANUFACTURED IN CHINA
10 9 8 7 6 5 4 3 2 1   First Edition

ROSA'S SONG

by
Helena Ku Rhee

illustrated by
Pascal Campion

RANDOM HOUSE STUDIO ⌂ NEW YORK

Jae was new to the country, the city, the building.

His family's apartment faced an alley, and Jae looked out the window. If he stared hard enough, would he be able to see his old village, his old home, his old friends?

No. He'd moved too far away.

His mother said, "You should go meet the other kids in the building."

"What if they don't like me? What if I forget my new words?"

"You won't know if you just stay here."

Jae put on his shoes and went downstairs
to the apartment below his. He rang the bell.

A girl opened the door. A colorful bird sat on her shoulder.

"Hi," she said. "I'm Rosa. This is my parrot, Pollito. It means little chicken."

Jae giggled. "Good name," he said, using the new words he'd learned.

Rosa asked, "Can I visit your apartment? I want to see where you live."

Jae started heading upstairs.
Rosa followed with Pollito on her
shoulder. Jae liked how friendly
Rosa was, and how Pollito nestled
by her ear.

Inside, Jae turned to Rosa and said, "No shoes."
He removed his sneakers. Rosa did the same.
As Rosa looked around the apartment, her eyes
gleamed as if she'd discovered something amazing.
She studied a vase with a dragon, and colorful rice
cakes on the kitchen table.

Jae walked to the window. Where he was from,
you could see mountains everywhere.
"No mountains," he said.

Rosa climbed onto the sofa. She clawed a cushion and said, "I'm climbing up, up, up a mountainside. I'm heading for the clouds!"

She smiled at the ceiling. Jae thought he saw clouds up there.

Jae remained by the window. He glanced at the empty alley below. Where he was from, people sold fruits and vegetables on the street.

"No people," he said. "No food."

Rosa approached the window. "I smell roasted corn! And fresh strawberries. I hear music, too!"

Jae closed his eyes and imagined the scent of fresh fruit, the melody of a pretty song filling his ears and his chest.

Rosa went to a bookshelf. It held photos of Jae's
old seaside village. And a few of his old friends.
Jae suddenly felt so sad.

Rosa surprised him by leaning with her hands cupped against the wall. She whispered, "If you do this, you'll hear the sea."

Jae did the same. He heard a quiet ocean breeze. He smelled the saltiness of the sea.

"I'll be your friend," Rosa said. "Pollito, too."

Jae glanced around his small apartment. It didn't seem so boring or lonely anymore.

"Want to sing with Pollito?" Rosa asked.

She and Pollito sang, "*Cuando vuelo lejos, mi corazón se queda aquí.* When I fly away, my heart stays here." Rosa caressed Pollito's wings while they sang again and again.

During the following weeks, Jae and Rosa explored the apartment complex for lost llamas, golden Inca treasures, and a rainforest with parrots—like where Rosa was from.

They sang with Pollito, who always remembered the song Rosa had taught him. "When I fly away, my heart stays here."

The summer went by quickly, thanks to Rosa and Pollito.
Jae learned so many new words! He and Rosa shouted
"Cartwheel!" on the grass and "Sunset!" at the sky.

One morning, Jae woke to find Rosa's colorful
bird in his apartment.
"Why is Pollito here?" he asked his mother.
"Rosa wanted you to have him."
Jae was startled. "But she loves Pollito!"

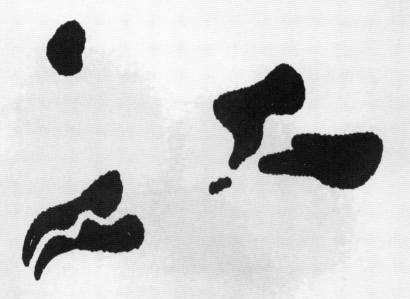

"Rosa and her family had to move away."

"Where?" Jae felt the tears coming.

His mother wrapped him in a hug. "Back to where they're from."

"But why didn't she tell me?"

His mother cried, too. "I don't think she knew. They had to leave quickly. They didn't have a choice."

Jae ran downstairs. Rosa's apartment was quiet.
He peered in the doorway. Nobody was inside.

Jae sat on the floor and cried.

A little while later, Jae went home. Pollito hopped onto Jae's hand and began to sing, "When I fly away, my heart stays here." But Jae couldn't sing. He didn't even feel like talking.

Someone knocked at the door.
A girl and boy stood in the hallway.
"Is that your bird?" the girl asked. "What's its name?"
"Pollito," Jae said. "Little chicken."
They giggled. Pollito started to sing again.
The boy asked, "Can you teach us the song?"
Jae nodded.

He remembered how Rosa would caress Pollito's wings while they sang, so he did the same. As the music filled his ears and his chest, he felt a little less lonely, a little less sad.

AUTHOR'S NOTE

I grew up in an apartment building near downtown Los Angeles, where people constantly moved in and out. Whether due to a family's change in financial status, marital status, or even immigration status, young friendships were often disrupted just as they were forming. I wrote this story because I remembered the loneliness that resulted from friends leaving suddenly, frequently without any warning. Thankfully, life always presented hope for new friendships and new beginnings, usually just a knock away.